THE STRAY DOGS

STRAY DOGS:
THE DEATH OF A DOG

Michael Choi

Michael Choi
2016

First Printing: 2016

ISBN 978-0-9951621-0-5

Michael Choi
76 River Grove Dr.
Toronto, Ontario M1W 3T9

Contact: thestraydogsproject@gmail.com

To myself,

for actually publishing a real book.

And to my mom, I guess.

Contents

ACKNOWLEDGEMENTS

I would like to thank my teachers, friends, and family who have been extremely helpful and supportive along this entire journey. I cannot begin to describe my love towards all of you. The amazing cover couldn't have been completed without the help from "Park Arts and Design" art school, for guiding me in making the greatest book cover. Without the guidance of my teacher, Jun Park, my cover would remain an underdeveloped idea on a piece of paper. Finally, I want to thank my English teachers. Without their push and demand for initiative, this entire project couldn't have been possible. It was only last year that I had developed the first rough copy of this book and submitted as a minor assignment to a particular teacher. Today, she still pushes to reach my maximum and beyond.

Preface: A Message

I am in grade 11 and barely surviving school. I have terrible habits in procrastination and lack of productivity. Also, I have the inability to focus on studies, so I participate in every single activity possible but studying; one activity in particular would be making a fricking book. Because I perform at maximum velocity when presented a challenge, I was able to ignore my terrible habits, laziness and procrastination to finally focus on publishing a damn book. Only last year I had reached the rougher copy of my project, and all who had read it suggested for me to publish the thing. So, like any sensible human being, I promised myself day to day for an entire year that I would publish the book. Well, I probably forgot about it within a month or two. Now, after procrastinating for a couple hundred days, it was my time to finally take action.

Jokes aside, I truly believe most people have had the thought of making a book of their own. After making mine, I now think it is something everyone should do. Humans have the inevitable ability to think different, every single mind comprehends differently and understands concepts only their own perspective is able to perceive. What I'm trying to say is that your mind is one of a kind, only one copy exists and thus the sharing of it through the pages of multiple novels is a stunning way of sharing the rarest treasure existing. Write a novel, about anything. Whether there will be readers is irrelevant, fame too is irrelevant. The idea is that you document a piece of your mind, that you create something that cannot be replicated. The idea is that you contribute to the world, a piece of yourself.

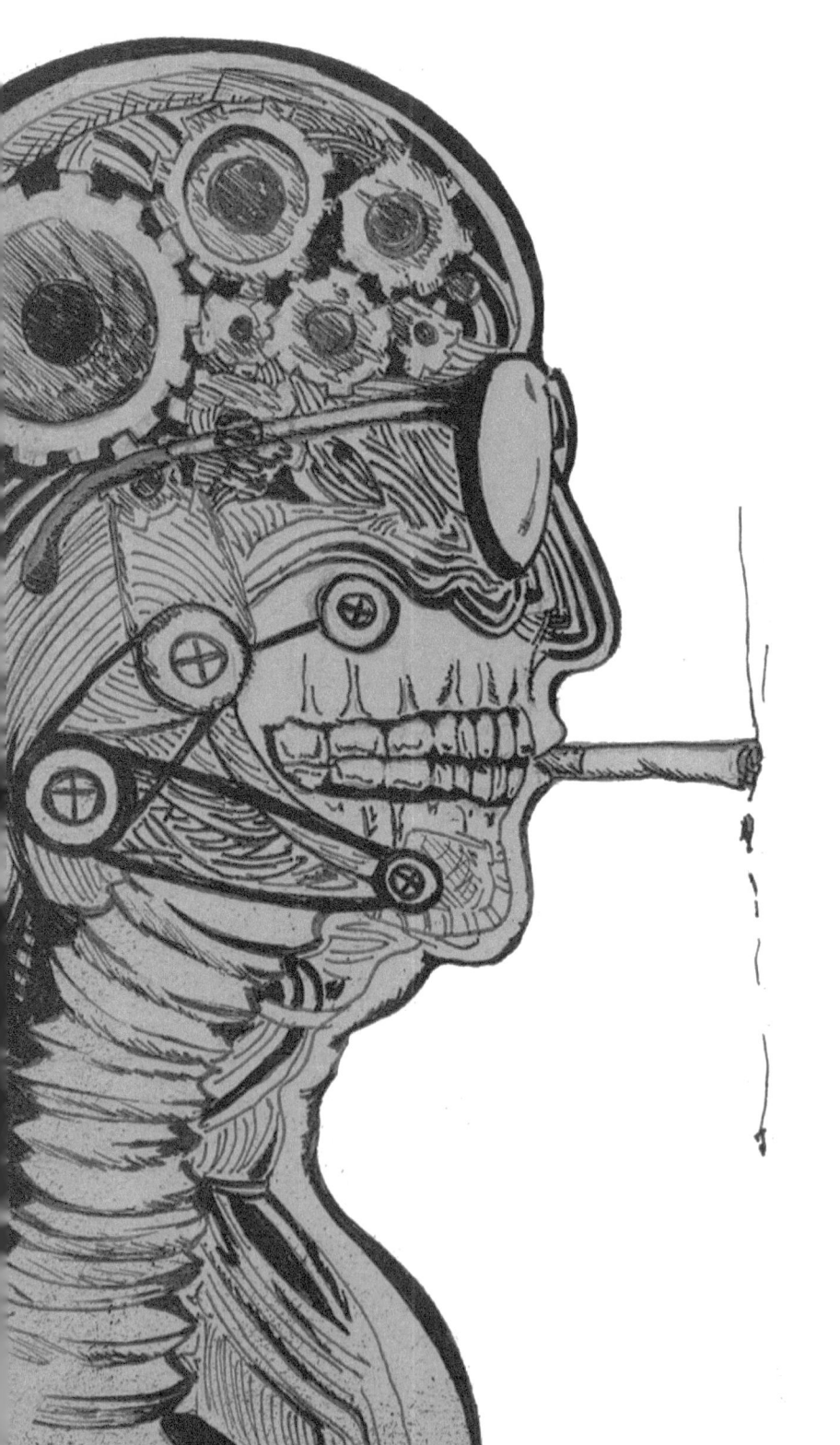

THE DEATH OF A DOG

Sometimes, I'd just stare. Waiting for something to happen, something to do. It would consume my youth, my prime of life. I spent hours before every night, waiting for the bloody thing to go off. I'd wake up with my chest pounding, to only face the horrific blank screen. It would lie on my hand and stare at me as if it would tick as it used to. Six long bloody years without any sign of life on the other end. I fell back to bed and thought about mama. I've begun to forget her face.

Sleep was impossible without two cups of vodka soiling my insides and tonight called for three. Rising from the creaky old bed, I made my way to the desk. I pulled out my bottle of remedy and drunk until the ground swayed. Navigating my way across the hardwood, I shuffled towards the balcony for a stick of smoke. "Arise ye workers, from your slumbers. Arise ye prisoners of want, ba da dum dum

dum..." The bloody song which threw flowers at Stalin was spouted from my mouth. "So comrades, come rally, and the last fight let us race. The Internationale unites the human race." Meeting the edges of my bottle to my loud mouth, I drunk carelessly as it soaked my chest.

"So, you've been drinking."

I rapidly turned towards the direction of his voice, smashing the bottle along the steel of the balcony. Flexing my fingers to tightly grip the pointed bottle, I allowed my training to trump over my drunkenness.

"Relax Feliks," said the young friend. "It's only me."

"Krovavyy durak (bloody fool). I would've sliced your stomach."

He laughed as he leapt from the edge and handed a Marlboro. He pulled his lighter from his pouch and opened the cap with one swift motion. Lighting his cigarette, he greeted the flame to mine as well.

"You drunk, you stupid drunk. You understand this is the worst time for a drink," he said dragging his cigarette.

"At night?"

"No, I mean the circumstances we're under." He blew towards to the moon and spoke softly as the smoke blurred his smooth face. We were similar of age, but his face resembled that of a child. The Marlboro made him the typical goon, a teen with a million ways to disappoint mothers everywhere. "I just came from Philly. I went to collect Petyr's intel." He masked his face in a cold and plain expression, but I knew he was aching inside. I felt the anger and pain brewing within his body. "He was found shot, and all his papers were gone."

My heart stopped. I looked at his scarred surface. He was fighting back tears. Personally, I rather loathed Petyr, but Stas loved him, they were comrades since their child-hood. They entered and exited the program together spending much of their lives following one another like thread and needle, inseparable. Stas' eyes glittered in the luminous moonlight, he sought comfort by toying with his lighter and smoked to occupy himself, to prevent the tears. "They took the intel?"

He fiddled with his lighter, the opening and closing of the cap made a distinct shriek which itched my ears. Then, he blew the long held smoke, and looked away as he brushed a tear. "No, Petyr burned them. He must've panicked; he burned himself badly before he got shot."

After a tense moment of silence, I reached within his leather jacket to find the familiar bottle which was always there. "Looks like you've been drinking too, you bloody hypo-crite." Raising the bottle until it covered the moon, I paid my respects to Petyr and emptied his whiskey. Then, after mak-ing conversations to further avoid tension, I said goodbye to

Stas before he leaped onto the roof and maneuvered his way across the city.

I was riled up from the whiskey so it ensured a certain amount of decent sleep. I killed the remainder my cigarette and sunk into bed once again. Before sleeping, I'd think about Stas. He grew up with a heavy knuckled father and relied on Petyr's family to care for him. Although I'd kill Petyr if it were up to me, I couldn't help being drowned in depression myself; he had lost more than a comrade, he had lost a brother, a feeling which was too familiar to me. I turned to my comfortable side and fell asleep viewing the traffic of New York.

Then, I saw it. I saw my life back in the program. My twelve year-old self, training and practicing for a lifetime of murder and hiding. General Vrasenko, the head director of the program watching our every move. There was my opponent, Stas. A fight which decided who was fit for the mission, a fight which only one exited. I had made it far, too far to lose now. I drew my knife, and he drew his. A twelve year old's hands wrapped around military grade knives, too heavy for men. We'd slash and weave, screaming sounds in accents terrible, until he'd find himself lying on the floor, my blade across his neck.

The general waited, waited for bloodshed. He was searching for something, he was looking inside me for re- morse, and I knew it. I pushed the blade down on his neck and prepared for a deep cut. As my muscles tensed and the knife was slightly stained, Stas did the unexpected, he cried. After years of teaching and programming to show no emo- tion, the boy had cried. Without thought, I released him and sheathed my blade. A hand struck me in my temple, and my stomach was met with a knee. "Gryaznyye trus (filthy cow- ard)," the general said. I looked up, and his face pierced my heart with a sudden wave of death and expressionlessness. He beat Stas all night, and sounds of cries and screams roared across the camp. The face of Vrasenko haunted me to this day.

I awoke to the unpleasant memory of Vrasenko's face, and there was a moment of panic before I re-focused on my surroundings. Out the window, the streets were less crowded and traffic was not as heavy, must be a Sunday. I reached for the covers that were piled at my feet and cloaked myself with it once more. Sleeping would help me sober up more, that whiskey still had me winded. But as always, the ticker gave me anxiety. So I reached for the plastic device once more and stared at the blank screen timelessly. Two years without a single message from the country, as if I'm forgotten, abandoned. "Negodyai (scoundrels). They poison the country from the heart."

I've always been loyal to my motherland, but I question their loyalty to me. They took away my childhood, my family and my life. I was robbed of my innocence, freedom, and youth to serve the country and they ignore me like a bastard son. These days, the only reason I'd get off bed every morn-ing is because of mama. Thinking of her, alone and worried restored my passion to execute their orders. Trying to re-member her face, I once again fell into memories.

I remembered the flame. The horrific flame which blind-ed the night still burned in my memories. We were all ready, it was the day we entered enemy lines. There we were, eighteen year-olds ready to face the world. The years of training and bloodshed finally led to the cold night in the Ovcharka air base. Before boarding the plane, Vrasenko lit flame to a puddle of gasoline. Confusion filled our hearts, all eyes were centered on the general. He stripped away our notebooks, dog-tags, and pictures, and tossed them all into the fire. Every picture of mama, every picture of me, and every picture which insisted that I exist was burned. He left me with a foreign passport, student ID and cards which sug-gested I had visited Disneyland. I still remember the photo; the fire was consuming the edges of the picture until she

8

was gone. The general faced us, his eyes covered under the shadow of death casted by his cap. With the click of his boot, he arched his back straight and saluted us. We boarded the plane, cramped up for hours until we reached America. I remember Stas fighting back tears, and Dimitri's song about the honor of death in war. I sang along loudly, proud to serve the motherland.

Knock. Knock.

I was startled. No one paid a visit in Sunday mornings and paranoia struck me down. I reached for my revolver holstered under the springs of my creaky bed. I steadied my sights towards the door.

"Feliks, it's me."

I foxed toward the door, opening it slightly to see the edges of Stas' figure. Opening the door, Stas entered with great anxiety. He was red, tense and panicked.

"Pack your gun and burn your intel," he said.

Immediately I reached for my suitcase and opened it. Stas came and joined me in ripping all the papers. "What's going on?"

"They've got 'em."

"Got who?"

"Dimitri! They've got Dimitri!"

"They killed him?"

"I dunno, but we need to get outta here."

We took our bits of paper and shoved them inside a trash can. Stas carefully and evenly soaked all the bits, and lit the papers. I readied my guns; one near my chest and one down my leg.

"The same ones who killed Petyr, they comin' for us too," he said running down the hall. "Dimitri didn't burn all his intel and they know where we are."

My ears rang as I ran down the steps. The elevator took too long, and so we scurried down the stairs. At basement, we entered the car and drove off into 56th street.

"They know why we're here, they know where we are, they know who we are, they know everything!" He was fiddling with his lighter again, and he began to receive calmness from it. "Alright, we're going to Philadelphia to get Leo and Sasha. We stay low in an inn on the way."

I nodded. I was paralyzed with the thought of capture, the thought of never seeing mama.

It was silent the whole ride down, and it was tough for me to maintain calmness. When we arrived at a motel, we did nothing but shuffle around the room in panic and thought. The TV only added to the mess, but it helped in slightly alleviating the ever so thick tension. Stas routinely peered through the blinds, his face was puddled with concern. I spent the night staring at the familiar blank screen of my ticker, waiting for something. It wasn't a mission I was waiting for, nor was it orders. I just wanted to know they were with me, they knew I existed, that they cared for my safety. I spun the device on my palm, flipping the device from its screen. There it wrote on the back, "soobshcheniye priyemnik (message receiver)." That was all I was. A pawn to their chessboard, nothing but a machine which executed their wants and goals. Anger consumed my heart and I tossed the device across the room.

"They don't care for us Stas, their world doesn't crumble if we die."

"What are you talking about?"

"Them you bloody idiot! Our country! They've forsaken us!"

"Have you lost faith in them? Millions have died to raise our country from ashes, and millions more raising the country to superiority! You talk like one of these American dogs, perhaps you've been blinded by them."

"You think they care for us? We're monsters to them, we're monsters to everyone. Whether you like it or not Stas, America is not the enemy. Neither is the state. We're stray dogs, we have no owners, we have no love, we have no will. Do you think they cared when Petyr died?"

Stas leapt towards me and threws a hard knuckle. Falling against the rough carpet, I spat the thick blood from my mouth.

"You filthy traitor. You stain the glory of the Union."

Overwhelmed with rage, I palmed the small revolver from my ankle. I stood in an immediate, single motion, the steel rested on Stas' forehead. I drew the hammer back that rang a cocking noise which washed the fear of God over Stas' face. His face was no longer of anger, but of a child's misery. With a sudden crippling force of guilt, I relieved the hammer into a safe position and threw the revolver across the room. I recollected my thoughts as my legs were defeated by gravity and an intense atmosphere of depression drowned me.

"I'm ready to die if I must. I just gotta see my mama."

Stas looked at me with eyes that resembled those of a toddler. He crumbled by the bed beside me and picked his jacket for a cigarette. We'd stare at the ceiling, held together with old paint and tape.

"We're all dogs Feliks. I'm a dog to the country, and I know it. The Union makes me feel like a pack, a belonging to a larger cause. It makes me, well, something. This bullshit we go through, it's not for me or you, or anybody else. It's for the future of our country, the future of the world."

He paused to drag his cigarette, and blew away to the ceiling. His face grew younger by each second.

"You realize this is what they want, dogs like you who focus on glory, honor, and the future. By the time you wake up, it's too late, and all you fight for is the past."

"Perhaps, but you're no better than me Feliks. You still are a dog to the world, you're still enslaved to impossibilities

that give you fake hopes. I hope you understand, you'll probably never see your mama anyway."

There was a long pause of silence, and my eyes grew
heavy. I knew he was right. He had to be right, but I'd never
accept it. The thought of mama gave me a reason to hold onto life, a reason to endure all the suffering.

Tick-tick-tick-tack-tick-tack-tick.

Povtoreniye, povtoreniye (repeat, repeat).

Tick-tick-tick-tack-tick-tack-tick.

Povtoreniye, povtoreniye.

For several moments, I had been confused to these
sounds. But as the repeating ticks and tacks began to famil-
iarize, it shocked my chest like heart was being squeezed. I
rose from my bed fast, and my head was rushed with blood.
Shaking off the slight faint, I walked towards the ticker
which lied on the coffee table. Following along my side was
Stas, equally shocked with fear and adrenaline.

The Death of a Dog

I held the ticker gently, my whole life trembled before the tiny device. My hands shook and my head was pounding, six years of loneliness and life consuming curiosities finally answered through a simple code of ticks and tacks. We heard each tick, decoding it within our mind. The message was short, and it simply said "loyal comrades, we understand your difficult times. We must have your full loyalty on these orders." Before anything else occurred, the ticks changed and a new message was received. We listened to it once, waiting to see how long it was. This message was long, and so we wrote it on the broken, cracked wall. Once all ticks and tacks were written, the entire wall was covered with dots and dashes. We began decoding once the ticker stopped.

I was always faster than Stas at decoding; I always was a rushed personality. Without completing the decoding, I took a few paces back to read the sentences produced. Stas was in the corner, completing the final bits. "The Americans wish to destroy our country through the capture and manipulation of you. To avoid this, you are ordered to complete the final precaution into ensuring the safety of Soviet Intelligence. Destroy all forms of intel, as well as the life of your own. For the great Union which generations have laid their lives for, I ask you our dear and loyal comrades to follow these steps of true loyalty..."

Little did I realize Stas was standing beside me, facing the horror of the wall. Stas' face was turning bright red, but his expression was calm. No longer did I see the toddler's eyes, or a child's innocent face. His face was mature and unreadable. The sign of life was lost from his eyes, and no emotion could be received from his cold figure. I began to feel a tone of death in the room and soon realized his face resembled the face of Vrasenko. The terrifying face of the general reflected through the once innocent face of Stas.

"Stas, please don't," I croaked.

The Death of a Dog

Without warning, Stas shoved me to the carpet and ran towards the end of the room towards the revolver. Pushing off the carpet, I lunged towards Stas to grab his legs. I caught Stas' leg, and pulled him in hopes of his fall. No, it was too late. He planted on the ground, but his hand held the revolver I had thrown only moments ago. My head was jerked to the ground as he pulled his leg away.

There was a moment of prayer when my head was down. A prayer to anything and everything that Stas didn't have the gun, a prayer that wished all this away. When I lifted my head, there was death greeting me through a black barrel held by the hands of Stas. No, not Stas, Vrasenko.

He looked at me straight into my soul, killing me with his words. "Feliks, this isn't about you. This isn't about me. Hell, this ain't about the bloody war. This is about loyalty, and the power loyalty brings to the future. We're all dogs to something, Feliks. Even you. I'm willing to die if it means I have a cause, a reason, an owner."

"Vy chertovski sobaka (you bloody dog). You foolish dog. Please! Stas, Please!"

A streak of tears fell from his cheek as he placed death on his temple. With one deep held breath, he pulled the trigger. The smoke covered his smooth face, the childish face of Stas. I turned away from the blood stained corpse. I was afraid, afraid of the lifeless body that stared back at me.

Sounds of car doors slamming echoed from outside the inn. I peered outside the blinds, bastards in black and white surrounding the filthy complex. I shuffled around the room, laughing, screaming, and crying.

"You worthless dog! You bloody worthless bastard!"

He wouldn't reply. The bloody idiot laid on the floor, his face painted in red.

I stared at the gun, its trigger seemed very friendly. It rested on Stas' hand, his small soft hand.

"I'm no dog. Stas, I'm no dog."

Heavy feet grew closer, five, maybe six men. I relieved my stomach from my belt and anchored it to the broken down fan. Dragging the brittle chair across the room, I'd think about mama again.

Truly, it wasn't the union's orders that had me jump, nor was it the fear of capture. I chose to jump, it was my decision. It was a way for me to be content with life, to die free from bullshit influences. Imagine if I fell to the Americans, it was inevitable I would break my loyalty. Well, I'd be their dog. I wish to die without a bloody leash around me; I wish to die free from restraint. I wish to die a human.

After all, I'm no dog.

NOTES

By now, you have reached the end of this short story. I am very open to criticism so please contact any suggestions and corrections to my email: thestraydogsproject@gmail.com

Also, I understand the poor level of Russian used in my story. I apologize to those who may have been offended by the poor use of Russian and feel free to contact me corrections of my poor Russian skills. Otherwise, thank you very much for reading my story, hope you enjoyed it!

GLOSSARY

Marlboro- a cigarette first introduced in 1924, it is now the

    best-selling brand of cigarettes worldwide

Ovcharka- a fictional airbase in which Feliks, Stas, Dimitri

    and others from the program rally to land in America.

    "Ovcharka" is also a Russian dog breed known to be

    alert, quick, fierce, and a favorable hunting dog

State- like "union," it is a common word for Soviet Russia

The Internationale- a French left-wing song which support-

    ed many socialist views, thus adapted by communist

    Russia as their national anthem until 1944

Ticker- a fictional device used to receive coded messages.

Similar to Morse code, the cypher consists of ticks and tacks

written as dots and dashes

www.ingramcontent.com/pod-product-compliance
Lightning Source LLC
Chambersburg PA
CBHW031905170626
46807CB00004B/1899